D0730325

CARTER HIGH®
M Y S T E R I E S

LIBRARY BOOK
Mystery

By Eleanor Robins

SADDLEBACK
EDUCATIONAL PUBLISHING

CARTER HIGH®
M Y S T E R I E S

Art Show Mystery
Aztec Ring Mystery
Drama Club Mystery
The Field Trip Mystery
Library Book Mystery

Lucky Falcon Mystery
The Missing Test Mystery
The Secret Admirer Mystery
The Secret Message
Where Is Mr. Zane?

SADDLEBACK
EDUCATIONAL PUBLISHING
www.sdlback.com

Copyright ©2006, 2011 by Saddleback Educational Publishing
All rights reserved. No part of this book may be reproduced in any form or
by any means, electronic or mechanical, including photocopying, recording,
scanning, or by any information storage and retrieval system, without
the written permission of the publisher. SADDLEBACK EDUCATIONAL
PUBLISHING and any associated logos are trademarks and/or registered
trademarks of Saddleback Educational Publishing.

ISBN-13: 978-1-61651-564-5
ISBN-10: 1-61651-564-3
eBook: 978-1-61247-132-7

Printed in Malaysia

20 19 18 17 16   5 6 7 8 9

Chapter 1

It was Monday. Lin was in science class. Miss Trent was her teacher.

Miss Trent said, "I graded your science tests. And I'll give them back to you now. So you can find out what grade you got."

Lin thought she did well on her test.

Miss Trent gave Lin her paper.

Lin looked at her grade. She was right. She did do well on it.

Miss Trent gave Chandra her paper.

Chandra sat next to Lin. Chandra looked at her grade.

Then Chandra looked at Lin. She said,

"I got a ninety-five on my test. What did you get?"

"I got a ninety-eight," Lin said.

Lin always made the best grade in the class. And Chandra always made the second-best grade.

Miss Trent passed out the rest of the tests.

Then Miss Trent said, "You have to write a paper for this class. It should be five pages long. And it should be about a science topic."

"When's the paper due?" Lin asked.

"Friday of next week, Lin," Miss Trent said.

Chandra said, "That doesn't give us much time."

Miss Trent looked at Chandra. But she didn't say anything to her.

Miss Trent went to her desk. She picked up some papers. Then she said,

"This is a list of topics. Pick one on the list. But only one student can write about each topic."

Miss Trent quickly passed out copies of the list.

Then she said, "Read the topics. I'll give you a few minutes to do that. Then I'll call the roll. And you can tell me the topic you picked."

Lin looked at the topics. She knew about some of them. But she didn't know all of them.

Chandra looked at the list, too. Then she looked at Lin.

Chandra asked, "Which will you pick?"

Lin said, "I don't know yet. But it will be something I want to learn more about."

Lin looked at the topics for a few more minutes. Then she picked one she liked.

Miss Trent called the roll. And the students told her which topic they had picked for their papers.

Miss Trent said, "Lin, your turn."

Lin told Miss Trent what she'd picked.

Miss Trent laughed.

Then Miss Trent said, "I should've known you would pick that, Lin. That's a hard one. It won't be easy to find books about that. But I know you can do it. You always like to do hard work."

That made Lin feel very good.

Then Miss Trent said, "Chandra, it's your turn."

Chandra said, "I was going to write about that, too. But Lin got to pick first. Now I'll have to pick something else."

"That doesn't matter. Just do a good job on your paper," Miss Trent said.

Chandra looked at the list. Then she picked a different topic.

Lin thought Chandra picked a good topic. But Miss Trent didn't say anything about it.

Miss Trent called the names of the rest of the students. And they told her what they'd picked.

Miss Trent said, "You might not find out a lot about your topic. So you might have to pick another one."

Lin hoped she could find a lot.

"You have only two days to pick a different topic. You can't change after that," Miss Trent said.

The bell rang.

Miss Trent said, "See you tomorrow. And don't forget to start to work on your papers."

All of the students had lunch next. They could leave their books on their desks until after lunch. It was okay with Miss Trent for them to do that.

Lin left her books on her desk. She started to walk to the door.

Lin wasn't in a hurry to leave. But Chandra was. And Chandra bumped into Lin.

Chandra said, "Lin, watch where you're going."

Chandra sounded mad. And she seemed mad, too.

Lin hoped Chandra wasn't mad at her. But why would Chandra be?

Chapter 2

Lin got to the lunchroom. She hurried inside. She got her lunch. Then she looked for her friends.

She saw Paige, Logan, and Drake. They sat at a table.

Lin lived at Grayson Apartments. The other three lived there, too. All four rode the same bus to school. And they were all good friends.

Lin hurried over to their table. She quickly sat down. She told them she had to write a paper for science.

Logan said, "I'm glad I don't have

Miss Trent for science. I don't like to write papers."

"Me neither," Drake said.

"What are you going to write about?" Paige asked.

Lin told her.

"I've never heard of that before," Paige said.

"It's new to me, too. That's why I picked it. I want to learn about something new," Lin said.

Jack came over to their table. Willow did, too.

Jack and Willow also lived at Grayson Apartments. Jack rode the bus with Lin and the other three. Willow rode a special bus with a wheelchair lift.

Lin told Jack and Willow about her paper. And she told them the topic she'd picked.

Then Lin said, "I want to go to the

library today. But I don't have time to go before school is out. I hope I find out a lot," Lin said.

Jack said, "I'll be glad to drive you to the town library. We can go after school. Just say the word. And I'll take you today."

Jack was the only one of them who had a car. It wasn't much of a car. But Jack liked to show it off. So he was always glad to take them somewhere.

"Thanks, Jack. I want to get started on my paper. But I can't go today," Lin said.

"I'll be glad to look up something for you. I can do that today," Willow said.

Willow loved books. She wanted to become a librarian. So she worked at the town library some days after school and some weekends.

Lin asked, "Will it be okay for you to do that?"

Willow said, "Sure. I just need work

while I'm there. I'll look for some books for you on my break. And I'll call you tonight. And let you know what I find."

"Thanks," Lin said.

Lin was glad Willow would look at the town library for her. Maybe Willow would find something there to help her. Lin hoped she did.

Later, Willow looked for some books for Lin. But Willow didn't find what Lin needed. Lin found that out when Willow called her later that night.

Willow said, "I looked up that topic for you, Lin. I found some books. They had a few bits of news. But not anything that would help you a lot."

"Thanks for looking for me, Willow," Lin said.

"Sure, any time," Willow said. "Will Miss Trent let you do research online?" Willow asked.

"No," said Lin. "She wants us to find books in the library."

Lin would have to find a book at the school library. Or she would have to write about something else. And she didn't want to do that.

Chapter 3

It was the next day. Lin was in science class. It was almost time for class to start.

Chandra came over to her desk.

"I found what I need for my paper. Did you find what you need for your paper?" Chandra asked.

Lin said, "Not yet. Willow looked in the town library for me. It doesn't have a lot about my topic. And I haven't had time to go to the school library. I hope I find a lot there."

"You might have to write about something else," Chandra said.

"I know. But I sure hope not, Chandra," Lin said.

The bell rang. It was time for class to start. Miss Trent called the roll.

Then Miss Trent said, "Today we'll go to the library. That will give you a chance to look up your topic. And maybe check out some books."

Lin was glad to hear that.

Miss Trent said, "We'll go now. So don't talk in the hall. And whisper when we get there."

The students went to the library.

Lin started to look for a book. She looked for a long time. She found some books. But they wouldn't help her very much.

Chandra walked over to Lin. She asked, "Did you find what you need for your paper?"

"Not yet. And I'm not sure I will," Lin said.

"That's too bad," Chandra said. Then she walked away.

It was almost the end of class. And then Lin found a book. It was just what she needed for her paper. Lin quickly checked the book out.

Lin wanted to show the book to Miss Trent. So she started to walk over to Miss Trent.

Chandra hurried over to Lin. "Did you find something you can use for your paper?" she asked.

"Yes," Lin said.

"Let me see it," Chandra said.

Lin showed her the book. But she didn't know why Chandra wanted to see it.

The bell rang.

Lin had to go to lunch. So she didn't have time to show the book to Miss Trent.

But that was okay. She could show the book to Miss Trent later.

Lin got all of her things. She walked to the door. Chandra did, too. Chandra was in a hurry. She bumped into Lin.

Chandra said, "Watch what you're doing, Lin. And don't bump into me."

Lin wanted to say she didn't bump into Chandra. But Chandra sounded mad. Was Chandra mad at Lin?

Chapter 4

It was the next day. Lin was in science class. It was almost time for class to start.

Lin wanted to show her book to Miss Trent. But Chandra said something to Lin before she could.

Chandra asked, "Did you get a lot done on your paper last night?"

Lin said, "No, I didn't. I had to study for a math test. But I hope to get a lot done on it tonight."

Chandra didn't seem mad. So it must be a good day for Chandra. And Lin was glad about that.

Lin asked, "How about you? Did you get a lot done on your paper?"

"Yes," Chandra said.

The bell rang. And Miss Trent started class.

Then Miss Trent said, "You can work on your papers all period. You can start on them now. You need to work. Don't talk to each other. This isn't a free period."

That was okay with Lin. She didn't want to talk. She just wanted to work on her paper.

Miss Trent said, "I'll call each of you to my desk. And you can tell me about the books that you found. But first, does anyone need to pick another topic? Today is the last day you can do that."

No one needed to do that. So all of the students got busy. Or at least they acted as if they were busy.

The students went over to Miss Trent,

one at a time.

Then Miss Trent said, "Lin, it's your turn."

Lin walked over to Miss Trent. She had her library book.

"This is what I found, Miss Trent," Lin said.

Lin gave her book to Miss Trent. Miss Trent looked at the book. Then she gave it back to Lin.

Miss Trent said, "I'm glad you picked your topic, Lin. You should learn a lot about it from this book."

"I hope I do," Lin said. And Lin thought she would.

Miss Trent said, "I'll enjoy reading your paper, Lin."

That made Lin feel very good. And she was glad she picked that topic.

Lin went back to her desk. She worked some more on her paper.

Then the end of class bell rang.

Miss Trent said, "Time to go. Don't forget to work on your papers tonight."

Lin got up to go to lunch. She left her books on her desk. Lin walked to the door.

Chandra seemed like she was mad again.

But Lin didn't know why. Lin hadn't done anything to Chandra. So Chandra couldn't be mad at her. Maybe it was just a bad week for Chandra.

Chandra wasn't in a hurry to leave. And Lin was glad. She didn't want Chandra to bump into her again.

Lin walked into the lunchroom. She got her lunch. Then she saw Paige and Willow. They were at a table.

Lin hurried over to their table and sat down.

Willow asked, "Did Miss Trent let you work on your paper today?"

Lin said, "Yes. And I got a lot done."

"Good. Maybe you'll finish it this weekend," Paige said.

"I hope so. But I need to get a lot done tonight," Lin said.

The girls started to talk about other things. And they talked too long.

Then Paige asked, "What time is it? I left my watch at home."

Lin looked at her watch. She said, "Oh, no. We need to go. Or we'll be late to class."

Lin quickly got up from the table. She took her tray back. Then she hurried into her science class to get her books.

Lin was in a hurry to go to her next class. So she didn't make sure all of her books were on her desk. She just quickly put them in her backpack.

Lin didn't think about the book she needed for the science report again until she got home. Then she looked in her backpack to get her book. It wasn't there.

Someone had taken her book when she was at lunch.

But why would someone steal her book? No one else needed it for the science report.

Chapter 5

It was the next morning. Lin was at the bus stop. Paige was there. Logan and Jack were there, too.

Lin was very upset. She didn't know where her book was. And she didn't get to work on her paper the night before.

Logan said, "You don't look so good, Lin. What is wrong with you?"

Lin wanted to do well in school. So she always worried.

"Are you sick?" Paige asked.

Lin said, "No, Paige. But I'm in big trouble."

Maybe it wasn't big trouble for Paige.

But it seemed like it was to Lin.

"Why? What did you do, Lin?" Logan asked.

"I didn't do anything," Lin said.

"So what's the problem then?" Logan asked.

"That book I checked out of the library. The one for my paper... I can't find it. And now I can't work on my paper," Lin said.

"When did you first miss the book?" Paige asked.

Lin said, "Last night. When I got ready to work on my paper."

"Did you look all around your house for it?" Paige asked.

"Yes. That's what I would have done," Jack said.

"I didn't need to do that. I just opened my backpack. And my book wasn't there," Lin said.

"Where was the last place you saw

it? Maybe you didn't take it to school yesterday," Logan said.

Lin said, "I did take it. I showed it to Miss Trent. And I used it to work on my paper in class."

Paige said, "You just took it to some other class. So your book must be in that class."

"Yeah, you just forgot where you left it," Logan said.

"For sure," Jack said.

"No. I didn't take it to another class. I think someone took it," Lin said.

They all seemed surprised.

"That's a dumb thing to say, Lin. Why would someone take your book?" Logan asked.

"Why would someone take your book?" Jack asked.

"I don't know. But I think someone did," Lin said.

"You must be wrong, Lin. You're the only one who needs it. You must have put it somewhere. And you just forgot where," Paige said.

Lin said, "No, I didn't. My book was on my desk when I went to lunch. It was gone when I got back."

"You should've said something then," Logan said.

"That's what I would have done," Jack said.

"I told you. I didn't know it was gone until I got home," Lin said.

"Then it has to be at school. In a classroom. Or maybe someone picked it up. But they didn't mean to do that," Paige said.

"Yeah," Logan said.

"Just say the word," said Jack. "And I'll help you look for it."

"Thanks, Jack," Lin said.

"We'll all help," Paige said.

"And I'll tell Drake and Willow, too," Jack said.

"Tell us the name of the book. So we'll know what to look for," Logan said.

Lin told them. Then Lin said, "We have to find it. I really need it to make a good grade on my paper."

The bus came. And they climbed onto the bus.

"Don't worry, Lin. One of us will find your book," Paige said.

"Yeah," Logan said.

"For sure," Jack said.

Lin knew they didn't think someone stole the book. They thought she just left it somewhere. And she just forgot where she left it. So they thought the book wouldn't be hard to find.

Chapter 6

The bus got to school. Lin got off the bus. She hurried into the school. She wanted to see Miss Trent before school started.

Lin walked quickly down the hall.

Chandra called to her. "Why are you in a hurry, Lin? Where are you going?" she asked.

"I want to see Miss Trent," Lin said.

"Why?" Chandra asked.

But Lin wanted to see Miss Trent. And she didn't have time to tell Chandra.

Lin got to Miss Trent's room. Miss Trent was there. And Lin was very glad.

Lin said, "I need to talk to you, Miss Trent."

Miss Trent said, "You seem upset, Lin. What's wrong?"

"My book is missing. The one I need for my paper," Lin said.

Lin didn't want to say it was stolen.

Miss Trent seemed surprised.

Miss Trent said, "I'm very surprised, Lin. You're a very good student. And I never thought you would lose a book."

"I didn't lose it. Someone took it," Lin said.

She still didn't want to say someone stole it.

Miss Trent seemed even more surprised by what Lin said.

Miss Trent said, "I can't believe someone would take your book. Why do you think that, Lin?"

"The book was on my desk when I went to lunch. It was gone when I got back," Lin said.

"Why didn't you tell me then?" Miss Trent asked.

"I didn't know it was missing then. I didn't miss it until I got home," Lin said.

"Then you don't know when you lost it," Miss Trent said.

Lin wanted to tell Miss Trent again that she didn't lose it. But she didn't. She knew Miss Trent wouldn't believe her.

"You must have left it somewhere, Lin. Look for it in your other classes. And maybe you'll find it. And look again at home. It might be there," Miss Trent said.

Lin knew it wasn't at home. And she knew it wasn't in her other classes.

Someone took it. But who? And why did the person take it?

But most of all, where was her book?

Miss Trent said, "I'll tell all of my students about your book. And I'll ask if they've seen it. They'll let you know if they know where it is, Lin."

"Thank you, Miss Trent," Lin said.

But Lin didn't think that would help her much.

Lin was worried only one person knew where the book was. And that was the person who stole it. Lin didn't think that person would tell where it was.

"What am I going to do? Can I pick someone else to write about, Miss Trent?" Lin asked. Lin didn't want to do that. But she knew she should.

Miss Trent said, "I'm sorry, Lin. But it's too late for you to do that. Yesterday was the last day to change your topic."

But Lin had to write about something else for her paper.

Lin said, "But I don't have my book. And I need it to get a good grade on my paper."

"I'm sorry, Lin," Miss Trent said. And she did seem sorry. "I can't let you pick something else. That wouldn't be fair to your classmates. You lost your book. They didn't lose their books."

Lin went to the door. She was very upset now. She had to find her book.

Lin walked out in the hall. She saw Chandra. Chandra was standing just outside Miss Trent's room.

Lin almost bumped into her. Chandra had a big smile on her face.

Chandra said, "So you lost your book. Too bad." But Chandra didn't seem like she thought it was too bad.

Lin started to say she didn't lose her book. That someone took it. But Chandra spoke before she could.

Chandra said, "You always make the best grade. But this time you won't, Lin. Not without that book."

Chandra still had a big smile on her face. Then Chandra hurried off.

Chandra must have stolen the book. Lin was almost sure about that.

But she didn't think Chandra would say she did. And Lin couldn't prove it. So how could Lin get her book back from Chandra?

Chapter 7

Later that morning, Lin was in the lunchroom. She looked for her friends.

Lin saw Logan. He was at a table with a girl. She must be his new girlfriend. Logan liked to date many girls.

Then Lin saw Willow and Paige. They sat at a table. Drake and Jack were also with them.

Lin got her lunch. Then she hurried over to the table and sat down.

Willow asked, "Did you find your book, Lin?"

"No," Lin said.

Paige said, "Sorry, Lin. I asked around.

But I didn't find out anything about your book."

"And I looked in all the desks I saw," Jack said.

"Me, too. And I also looked in the gym," Drake said.

"Thanks to all of you for the help. We didn't find my book. But I might know who took it," Lin said.

"Who did?" all four asked at the same time.

Lin told them she talked to Chandra. And she told them what Chandra had said about her book.

"Chandra must have taken it," Drake said.

"For sure," Jack said.

Willow said, "You shouldn't say that, Jack. She might have taken it. But we don't know that for sure."

"What can I do? Just say the word. I'll do it," Jack said.

"Just keep looking for my book. And ask some more people about it," Lin said.

"We will, Lin. And we'll find it," Paige said.

"Yes, we will," Willow said.

But Lin didn't think they would. Not before her paper was due.

Paige said, "We can hurry and eat. And then go and talk to people about the book."

"That sounds like a plan to me," Drake said.

"And to me," Jack said.

They all ate quickly. And they didn't talk.

Then all five left the lunchroom. Lin and Willow went out into the hall. They hurried down the hall. They saw Chandra.

She was walking in front of them.

Willow said, "Wait, Chandra. We want to talk to you."

Chandra stopped. Then she turned around to face them.

Chandra asked, "What do you want? I didn't do anything wrong."

"I didn't say you did," Willow said.

"So what do you want?" Chandra asked.

Willow said, "Lin can't find her library book. Do you know where it is?"

"How would I know? Lin needs to keep track of her books. Maybe then she wouldn't lose them," Chandra said.

"I didn't lose my book. Someone took it," Lin said.

Willow said, "That's right. And we thought you might know who took it."

"How would I know?" Chandra asked.

"Maybe because you took it. Then Lin

wouldn't get a good grade on her paper. And you would get the best grade, not Lin," Willow said.

Chandra looked at them. She seemed mad. At first, she didn't say anything.

But then Chandra said, "Maybe I took the book. Maybe I didn't. But what if I did? You can't prove it. And you'll never find it. Not where I would have put it."

Then Chandra hurried off.

"She took it. I know she took it," Lin said.

"I think she did, too," Willow said.

"But how can we prove it?" Lin asked Willow.

"I don't think we can," Willow said.

"What am I going to do? I have to get my book back before next Friday," Lin said.

Willow said, "I know. But don't give up. We still have some time to look for it, Lin."

"But where is it?" Lin asked.

"I don't know. But we'll find it," Willow said.

They might think of somewhere else to look. But Lin didn't think her book would be there.

Chapter 8

Lin and Willow were still in the hall. They were trying to think of a place to look for Lin's book.

Willow asked, "Have you been to the library today, Lin? Have you asked about your book?"

"No," Lin said.

"We have some time before our next class. We can go there now. Maybe someone found your book. And turned it in," Willow said.

"Okay," Lin said.

The two girls went to the library.

Lin asked if her book had been turned

in. But it hadn't been turned in. That didn't surprise Lin. She didn't think it had been.

The girls left the library. They hurried down the hall.

Lin was sure she wouldn't find the book. So she wouldn't get a good grade on her paper.

Willow stopped her wheelchair.

Lin asked, "What's wrong, Willow?"

Willow quickly turned her wheelchair around. Then Willow said, "I have an idea. Come on."

Willow started to move her wheelchair quickly down the hall. Lin hurried to keep up with her.

"Where are we going?" Lin asked.

"To the library," Willow said.

"Why? We were just there. And no one had turned in my book," Lin said.

"And I don't think anyone will turn it in," Willow said.

"Why are we going back?" Lin asked.

Willow was in a hurry. So she didn't answer Lin.

The two girls got to the library.

Willow asked, "Do you know the call number of your book?"

"No," Lin said.

But Lin knew what a call number was. It let people know where a book could be found in the library.

Willow said, "Quick. Look up the call number of your book. Then write it down. And bring it to me. I can guess some of it. But I need to know all of it."

"Okay," Lin said.

Willow wheeled over to look at some of the books.

Lin quickly found the call number of

her book on the library's computer. And she took it to Willow.

Willow looked at the call number. Then she looked at the shelf in front of her.

"Found it," Willow said.

Willow got a book off of the shelf. She gave the book to Lin.

Lin couldn't believe it. It was her missing book.

"How did you know it was here?" Lin asked.

Willow said, "I didn't know for sure. But Chandra said it was somewhere we would never look."

And Lin would never have looked there at all.

"Chandra thought we would only ask if the book had been turned in. And we wouldn't look on the shelf. So I thought

Chandra might have put it here," Willow said.

"But how did you think to look here? I would never have thought to do that," Lin said.

Willow said, "I work in a library. I know that sometimes a book is on the shelf. But we think it's checked out. That doesn't happen a lot. But it's a good idea to look on the shelf. And make sure the book isn't there."

"I'm glad you work at the town library, Willow. So you knew to look on the shelf for my book. Chandra put the book on the shelf. But she didn't check it in. It was the perfect hiding place," Lin said.

Lin was sure Chandra put her book on the shelf. But Lin couldn't prove it. So she wouldn't say anything to Chandra about the book.

Lin was just glad that Willow found the book for her. Now she thought she would get a good grade on her paper for Miss Trent.